ON
THE
MOVE
Moving Trucks
SOLD

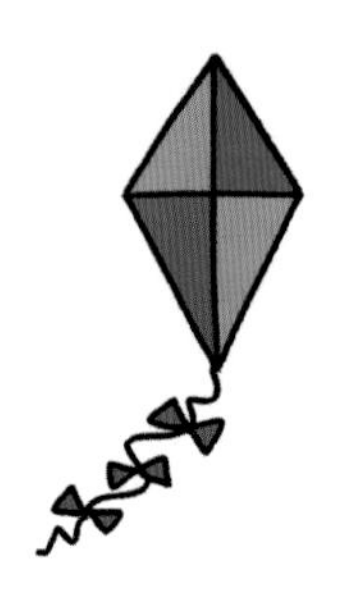

To Nana

BLOOMSBURY CHILDREN'S BOOKS
Bloomsbury Publishing Inc., part of Bloomsbury Publishing Plc
1385 Broadway, New York, NY 10018

BLOOMSBURY, BLOOMSBURY CHILDREN'S BOOKS,
and the Diana logo are trademarks of Bloomsbury Publishing Plc

First published in the United States of America in July 2022
by Bloomsbury Children's Books

Library of Congress Cataloging-in-Publication Data
Names: Frost, Maddie, author, illustrator.
Title: Iguana be a dragon / by Maddie Frost.
Description: New York : Bloomsbury Children's Books, 2022.
Summary: Iguana is worried he is not amazing enough to go to Cheetah's party,
but he soon learns that being himself is always enough.
Identifiers: LCCN 2021048230 (print) | LCCN 2021048231 (e-book)
ISBN 978-1-5476-0653-5 (hardcover) • ISBN 978-1-5476-0654-2 (e-book)
ISBN 978-1-5476-0655-9 (e-book)
Subjects: CYAC: Self-confidence—Fiction. | Individual differences—Fiction. |
Iguanas—Fiction. | Animals—Fiction. | LCGFT: Picture books.
Classification: LCC PZ7.1.F75584 Ig 2022 (print) | LCC PZ7.1.F75584 (e-book) | DDC [E]—dc23
LC record available at https://lccn.loc.gov/2021048230

The art for this book was created using a
Wacom tablet and digital brushes in Photoshop on a Mac
The story was typeset in Let's Draw Fun Animals, a font created by Maddie Frost
Book design by Jeanette Levy
Printed in China by Leo Paper Products, Heshan, Guangdong
2 4 6 8 10 9 7 5 3 1

To find out more about our authors and books visit
www.bloomsbury.com and sign up for our newsletters.

IGUANA BE A DRAGON

MADDIE FROST

BLOOMSBURY
CHILDREN'S BOOKS
NEW YORK LONDON OXFORD NEW DELHI SYDNEY

Iguana had just moved into a new house and . . .

He had mail.

You're invited to a

POOL PARTY!

@ 2:00 pm

Cheetah's House

(the ONE with the balloon)

Please RSVP

Coming

Not coming

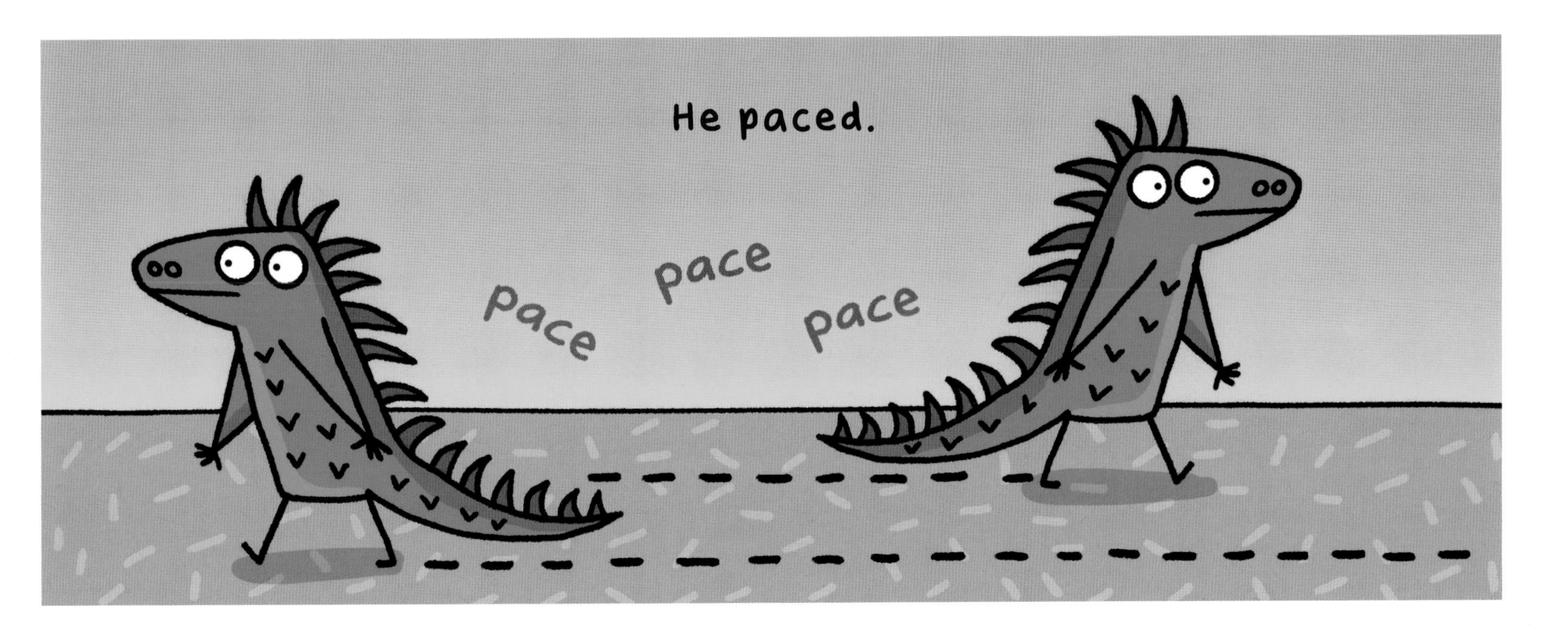
He paced.
pace
pace
pace

He stared.

He had never been to a pool party before.
LAMPS
But that wasn't the problem.

Cheetahs are the fastest animals in the world.

FASTEST

That makes them amazing.

He made a checklist:
Iguanas are green.

They enjoy the sun.
SCALE SCREEN
SPF 100

They're green.

I AM NOT

AMAZING!!!
You're invited to a
POOL PARTY!
@ 2:00 pm
Cheetah's House
(the one with the balloon)
please RSVP
Coming
Not coming

Maybe he could come up with something to really WOW the crowd.

Or he could just sit this one out.

PIZZA
He wasn't really in the mood to go swimming anyway.

DRAGON DONUTS
NOW OPEN!
BUMP
Then, out of nowhere, he got a sign.

GASP!
Dragons are amazing.
DRAGON DONUTS
NOW OPEN!

He made another checklist:
Dragons can fly:
Amazing.
They have magical horns
for doing magical things:
Very amazing.
MAGIC
MAGIC
MAGIC
They shoot blazing fire
out of their mouths:
EXTREMELY AMAZING!

He went straight to Sweet Deals Thrift Shop to find something that would make him look like a dragon.

No.

No.

No.

Maybe? No, no.
Definitely not.

Hmm . . .

BOOP
Boop
TIE
TIE
TIE

PERFECT!

Well . . . he would get used to it.
There was just one thing missing . . .

First, he tried some vegetarian chili.
Careful. It's spicy!
WOW! THAT'S SPICY!
MENU
• Hot fries
• Spicy Kale Kebab
• buffalo cauliflower
• Veg. Chili

Next, some buffalo cauliflower.
X-TRA HOT

To finish, the "I'm Feelin' Hot-Hot-Hot" spicy kale kebab.

Iguana breathed.
Hhhhhh
No fire.

HHHHH!
Still nothing.

And then, he felt it.
Almost like a—

BURRRRP

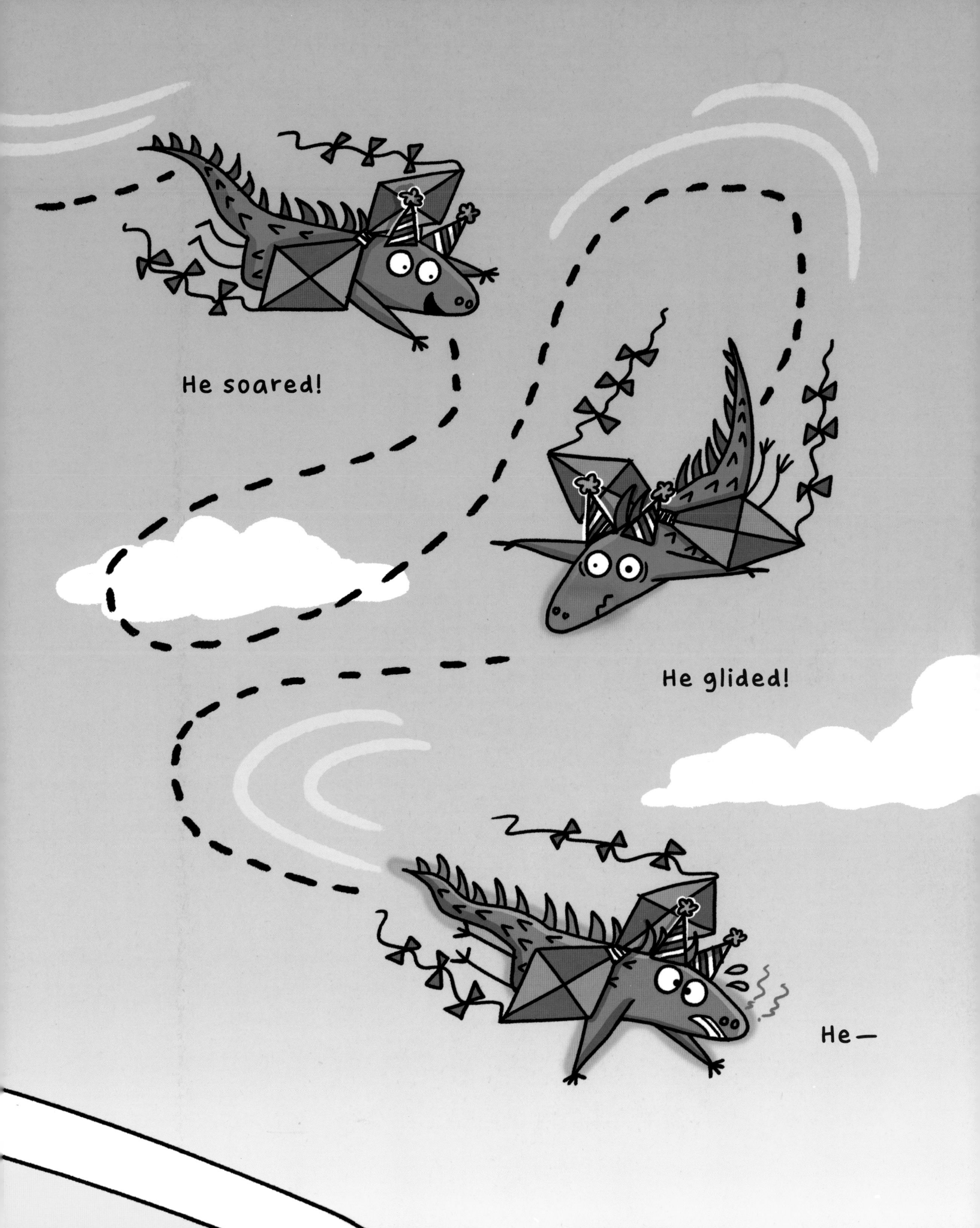
He soared!
He glided!
He—

Was hot!
Too hot!
He spun out of control!

He saw a pool in the distance
and braced for landing.

SPLASH

He swam as fast as he could to cool down.

That he had landed right in the middle of a race.
At Cheetah's pool party!

Cheetah was impressed.

As it turned out, there were a lot of amazing things about Iguana.

He was an
excellent climber.
YAY!

He told hilarious jokes.
And then the frog said, "Pineapple!"
BAHAHA

He was REALLY good at
hide and seek.

And he was super thoughtful.
Got the chips and dip!
Thanks, dude!

Iguana didn't need to worry so much
about fitting in . . .

He just needed to be himself.

Now that is pretty amazing!